Big Cowboy Western

Big Cowboy Western

To the Children of Elm Haven Housing Project

Big Cowboy Western

by Ann Herbert Scott

Pictures by Richard W. Lewis

Lothrop, Lee & Shepard Co., Inc.
New York

js 4253bi

Fourth printing, September 1967

It was Martin's fifth birthday.

His oldest sister Julia made him a chocolate cake with chocolate icing and a big five on top.

His next oldest sister Linda ran down to the corner store near the housing project where they lived and bought candles for the cake.

And his three other sisters, Olivia and Pearl and Cookie, giggled and whispered and spelled out words they knew Martin was too little to understand.

But *nobody* — not Julia or Linda or Olivia or Pearl or Cookie — would tell him what was in the mysterious box on the top shelf of his mother's closet.

Martin had guessed and guessed.

Was it a basketball he could bounce like the big boys on the playground below their apartment?

"Noooooo," said Julia and Linda and Olivia and Pearl and Cookie.

Was it a bag of candy with lollipops and bubble gum and jawbreakers and licorice sticks?

"Noooooooo," said his sisters.

Was it a spaceman's suit with a magic helmet and a special window in the front?

"Noooooooooooooo," they all said again.

Finally, Martin gave up guessing. "You'll just have to wait till Mommy comes home from work," Julia told him. "Then you can open the box and find out for yourself."

Martin waited for what seemed like a very long time. Then there was the clickety-clack sound of his mother's heels on the stairs and the snap of his mother's key in the door.

"Well, there's my birthday boy!" Martin's mother said as she picked him up and gave him a hug and six kisses — one for each year he'd lived and one to grow on.

Then she went to the closet and took down the mysterious box and said, "Happy birthday, son."

Martin grabbed the box and tore off the bow and the wrapping paper. And what did he find inside?

Not a basketball like the big boys played with.

Not a sack of candy.

Not a spaceman's suit.
But a cowboy hat and a holster with two silver guns.

"Wow," said Martin. "Wow, wow!"

Then instead of saying thank you to his mommy and his sisters, who were all standing around in a circle watching, Martin took out his guns and shot them off into the air, "Pow, pow, POW!"

"You look like a real cowboy, honey," Martin's mother said.

"I *am* a real cowboy," said Martin. "I'm Big Cowboy Western."

Martin's five sisters began to laugh.

"Oh, Martin, you're so silly," said Julia.

"You're way too little to be a real cowboy," said Linda. "Why you're the littlest in the whole family."

"Even littler than me," said Cookie.

"Pow, pow, POW!" Martin shouted, throwing his hat into the air and shooting at it with one gun.

"And all that noise doesn't make you a real cowboy, either," said Olivia. "What makes a *real* cowboy is having a horse."

"That's right, Martin," said Pearl. "Who ever saw a real cowboy without a horse?"

"Pow, pow, pow," said Martin, shooting with both guns but not so loudly as before. "Just you wait. Big Cowboy Western will find his horse."

That night when his mother came to tuck him in bed, Martin put both his guns under his pillow and hung his hat on the bedpost.

"Good night, little Martin," his mother said, giving him a hug.

"But I'm *not* little Martin. I'm Big Cowboy Western. Be careful not to step on my saddle."

"I'll be careful, son," his mother said as she switched off the light.

The next day when his mother had gone off to work and all his sisters were going off to school, Martin went across the hall to Aunt Sadie Miller, the lady who took care of him till his sisters came home in the afternoon.

"Why, Martin," Aunt Sadie said when he came through the door, "if you're not the cutest thing! What's a little fellow like you doing with those big guns? Too bad you don't have a little old rocking horse to ride."

Martin did not smile at Aunt Sadie. "I'm Big Cowboy Western," he said. "Can't you tell?" Then he got out one of his guns and aimed it at Aunt Sadie's geranium plants. "I can shoot anything with my guns. Just watch. Pow! Pow! Pow!"

"Now, little Martin. Don't go making all that noise in here," Aunt Sadie warned. "You go play your game outside."

"But I'm *not* little Martin. Can't you see that I'm Big Cowboy Western!" Then he took the piece of bread and jam that Aunt Sadie had fixed for him and said, "I think Big Cowboy Western will go look for his horse outside."

"Look all you want, honey," Aunt Sadie called after him. "Just be careful not to cross the street."

Martin went down the four flights of stairs and out in back of the project by the playground. It was a bright sunshiny day. He took his guns from his holster and shot them both at once at the sun. "Pow," he said, "pow, pow, pow, pow, pow!"

"Yaaaaannh, look at that," said one of the big boys who were bouncing a basketball against the side of the building. "Look at that little fancy pants. Isn't he tough, though?" Then they all started to laugh. "Funny little kid making out he's some hotshot cowboy."

"I *am* a cowboy. I'm Big Cowboy Western," Martin shouted and shot off both his guns again, "Pow, pow, pow, pow, POW! And Big Cowboy Western doesn't like anybody to laugh at him."

"Better tell that to your horse, fancy pants."

Martin went around from the back of the building to the front. Nobody was there, so he sat down on an empty bench. He aimed his gun at the quilt which was hanging over a balcony. "Pow, pow, pow," he said sadly.

"Well, look who's here," a voice surprised him. He looked up to see old Mr. Arrico, the fruit and vegetable man who came to visit Aunt Sadie each morning.

"Hi," said Martin. "I'm Big Cowboy Western."

"So I noticed," said Mr. Arrico. "Did you just get to town?"

"Just last night," said Martin.

"Do you think you'll like it here in the big city?" Mr. Arrico asked.

"Pow," said Martin, "pow, pow, pow," aiming at the red tassels on the harness of Lady, Mr. Arrico's horse.

"I guess you know all about what cowboys do."

"Big Cowboy Western knows just about everything," said Martin.

"I guess he knows how to take care of horses . . . that's what cowboys generally do on ranches."

Martin nodded yes.

"I guess he must miss his horse something awful."

Martin nodded again.

"Do you suppose he'd have the time to take care of my horse Lady while I go inside? You know Lady comes from the West, too. And it's been a long time since she's had a cowboy to take care of her."

Martin smiled.

Then Mr. Arrico introduced Big Cowboy Western to Lady. He held him up so he could rub Lady's nose, the way cowboys know how to do. Lady looked pleased. So did Big Cowboy Western.

"Will you take good care of Lady?" Mr. Arrico asked as he got out a basket filled with oranges and bananas and yams and collard greens.

"Yes, sir."

"There's just one thing I'd better mention," said Mr. Arrico, tying Lady's reins to the telephone pole. "Lady's getting to be a pretty old horse and shooting guns makes her a little nervous. Do you suppose Big Cowboy Western could remember that?"

"Yes, sir."

So that morning and every morning about the same time, Big Cowboy Western took care of Lady in front of the project while Mr. Arrico went inside to sell his oranges and bananas and yams and collard greens.

Sometimes on Saturdays, when they were home from school, his sisters Julia and Linda and Olivia and Pearl and Cookie would stand and watch. And sometimes the little children, who were only one and two and three and four, would crowd around to see Big Cowboy Western and his horse.

But every morning, whether or not anyone else was there, Big Cowboy Western talked to Lady and rubbed her nose and switched away the flies.

And once in a while, in the most quiet way, Big Cowboy Western would take out his guns and whisper ever so softly, "Pow, pow, POW!"